7/05

Ray Romano

with **Richard** and **Robert Romano**   illustrated by **Gary Locke**

Raymie, Dickie, and the Bean

Why I Love and Hate My Brothers

A Byron Preiss Visual Publications, Inc. Book

Simon & Schuster Books for Young Readers

New York   London   Toronto   Sydney

To my kids: Ally, Greg, Matt, and Joe.

I hope I can make your childhood as joyful as you're making the rest of my life.

—R. R.

ACKNOWLEDGMENTS

There were a lot of people who helped make this book possible. I'd like to thank you all, including:

My brothers, Rich and Bobby. When we were growing up, we did a lot of laughing, fighting, hugging, and punching, and it was great doing all of that again while making this book. Although it's hard to write in a headlock, this was a true labor of love. I'd also like to thank my parents, Albert and Lucie, for giving us all a childhood we'd want to remember together.

Thank you to my manager, Rory Rosegarten; my agents, Mel Berger and Sam Haskell; my attorney, Jon Moonves; and my assistant, Christy Kallhovd.

Byron Preiss and Dinah Dunn and everyone at Byron Preiss Visual Publications for putting up with all of my changes, and the additional changes to my changes.

The whole gang at Simon & Schuster, and very special thanks to our illustrator, Gary Locke, who made us all look cuter than we really were.

And finally of course my wife, Anna, and the kids. I love you all.

Special thanks to Zack Jenis, Luke Venditti, and Robert Romano for modeling for this book.

SIMON & SCHUSTER BOOKS FOR YOUNG READERS
An imprint of Simon & Schuster Children's Publishing Division
1230 Avenue of the Americas, New York, New York 10020
Copyright © 2005 by Sweaty Hugs, Inc.
Illustrations copyright © 2005 by Sweaty Hugs, Inc., and Byron Preiss Visual Publications, Inc.
All rights reserved, including the right of reproduction in whole or in part in any form.
SIMON & SCHUSTER BOOKS FOR YOUNG READERS is a trademark of Simon & Schuster, Inc.
The text for this book is set in Henman A Bold.
The illustrations for this book are rendered in oil paints.
Manufactured in the United States of America
2 4 6 8 10 9 7 5 3 1
CIP data for this book is available from the Library of Congress.
ISBN 0-689-86451-5

first edition

Hi. My name is Raymond.
I'm ten years old.

My older brother is twelve. His name is Richard, but everybody calls him Dickie. He likes that now, because he's twelve.

My younger brother, Robert, is four years old. We call him Bean, because of the shape of his head. We think he likes that, although he's never told us so.

They both call me Raymie—to my face, at least.

Sometimes I love my brothers.

Sometimes I hate them.

Today Mom and Dad are taking us
to the amusement park.
Mom says we can go
as soon as everyone's dressed.
Bean doesn't know how to dress himself,
so Dickie and I have to help him.

The three of us climb in the back of the car
and wait for Mom and Dad.

We wait

and wait

and wait.

Finally, after what seems like four hundred hours, they get in the car and we are on our way.

Dickie is so excited that he gives me some noogies.
I hate that, but he and Bean think it's hilarious.

On the car ride I tell a really funny joke.
"How do you make an elephant float?
You get a cup and . . . um, uh, a cup . . .
you put . . . no, wait . . . uh . . . you put stuff
in a cup and add two scoops of elephant."

Dickie says my jokes are stupid, but Bean likes them. He always does.

When we get to the park, Mom tells Dickie he has to hold Bean's hand. Dickie hates that, because I get to run ahead.

"So long, suckers!"

Dickie and I want to run right to our favorite ride, the Vomitizer. But Mom makes us go on Chuckie the Choo-Choo with Bean first.

Then Dickie and I go on the Vomitizer. We like going together because then we're not scared.

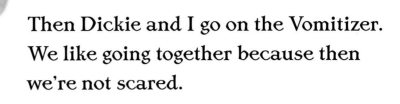

Dad buys us hot dogs for lunch.

Good thing about eating with Bean:
He can never finish his food.

Bad thing about eating with Bean:
Food makes him stinky.

After lunch we play a lot of games.

At the Magic Show the magician picks Dickie to be his assistant and gives him a magic wand.

Dickie starts poking me with the wand because he knows I want it.

I tell him, "I guess the wand's not really magic, because you're still ugly."

Then Mom gets us some cotton candy. Mom won't let me eat mine after I drop it on the floor.

I hate Dickie because he thinks it's funny, but Bean just thinks it's sad.

When no one's looking, I eat some anyway. Bean's the only one who sees it, but he won't tell.

Then we head out to Roaring River.

While we are on line, Bean starts jumping up and down, which can only mean one thing: Mom is going to make one of us take him to the bathroom.

"He can go on the ride. He's gonna get wet anyway," Dickie says.

"Can't he go in the bush? Dad did at the barbeque," I say.

"Raymie, just take your brother to the bathroom," Dad says quickly.

I take him quickly and wait outside the stall for him to finish.

"Raymie,
are you still there?"

"Yeah."

"Raymie,
you still there?"

"Yeah."

"Raymie,
you still there?"

"No."

"Hey! You didn't fool me
anyhow," Bean says.

I laugh at him and then help
him get dressed and head
back to Roaring River.

He's not a bad little brother.

Finally we go on Roaring River. Mom and Dad say it's going to be the last ride of the day, so we want to make sure we get soaked. We sit in the first car because that's where you get splashed the most. We talk Dad into buying us the picture they take on the final plunge.

Bean falls asleep in the car going home.

Sometimes I think he's faking it
so he doesn't have to carry anything in.

Dickie and I go to our room to split the winnings. It goes
well, until we get to the biggest one: the blue monkey.
I want it because monkeys are my favorite animal.
He wants it probably because he looks like one.

We spend some time discussing it.
Our discussion wakes up the Bean.

We can't let Bean tell Mom we woke him.

So we do what we have to do.

Finally it is time to go to bed.
Dickie has one last surprise waiting for me.
I hate sharing a room with him.

But when the lights go out, and the shadows start looking like monsters, I'm glad he's here.

Then I throw the sock on Dickie's head and go to Bean's room to get back my monkey.